THE PIED PIPER
OF
HAMELIN

RETOLD AND ILLUSTRATED BY
VAL BIRO

Oxford University Press

Once upon a time, long ago, there was a town called Hamelin. It was a lovely town, with a river on one side and a mountain on the other.

It had fine houses and shops. It had a church and a town hall. It even had a fat Mayor. So the people of Hamelin should have been happy — but they were not. They were utterly miserable. And what was it that made them so miserable?

RATS! Hamelin was absolutely full of rats.

They chased the people.

They fought
the dogs and cats.

They bit
the children.

They ate all the cheese
and they licked up the soup.

They gnawed people's
clothes

and crawled into their hats.

'Stop these rats!' cried the people as they flocked to the town hall. They were furious with the fat Mayor and his Corporation. 'DO something! If you don't rid us of rats, we shall get rid of YOU!'

The Mayor sat down with his Corporation. He groaned in despair because he did not want to stop being Mayor. But he had no idea how to rid Hamelin of rats. Neither had the members of his Corporation and they scowled wretchedly. Only the rats were happy.

Suddenly there was a tap at
the door. 'Another rat?' they
cried in alarm, as if there
weren't enough rats already.
But it was not.

It was a tall, thin stranger
in red and yellow, and he
had a reed pipe in his
hands. He spoke curiously:
'On this magical pipe
I can play a strong charm
To rid you of pests
That cause you alarm.
Be it rat or a bat
Or a toad or a viper
It will dance to the tune
Of the piping Pied Piper!'

The Mayor and Corporation were delighted.
Here was the perfect answer! They
surrounded the Pied Piper and promised him
anything as long as he got rid of the rats.

The Pied Piper asked for a
thousand guilders as his fee.
The Mayor promised faithfully
to pay him that, and even more!

So the Pied Piper walked out into the Market Square,
followed by the awestruck Mayor and Corporation.
He began to play his pipe, and at the first notes
of his magical tune the strangest thing happened.

The rats of Hamelin came scampering out.
Every one of them! From houses and shops,
from cellars and roofs they came, dancing
to the tune of the piping Pied Piper.

He began to dance along himself, playing his magical tune.
The rats followed: black rats, brown rats, grey rats, fat rats,
father and mother rats, uncle and cousin rats, they all danced
after the Piper, entranced by his music.

The Mayor and Corporation and
the people of Hamelin stood by
in wonder, as if rooted to
the ground.

The children of Hamelin came running out.
Every one of them! Boys and girls, brothers
and sisters, big and small, fat and thin,
they all danced after the piping Pied Piper.
The Mayor and Corporation and the people of
Hamelin stood aghast to see their children
dancing away. The magical tune made them
stand bewitched, unable to move a step.

This time the Pied Piper went the other way and
he led the children to the mountain. When they
reached it, a great big cavern opened up and
the children danced through one by one.
And when the last child went through,
the cavern in the mountain closed and
the piping was heard no more.

The Mayor was terrified, as well he might be! The
people of Hamelin turned on him in fury.
'It's all your fault!' they shouted and they chased him
round the town and out through the gates.

There the Mayor was thrown into the river
and the Corporation tumbled and plunged in
as well, to be washed away by the swift waters.
Just like the rats.
And they were never seen again!

At that moment the tones of a pipe could be heard once more,
and the people looked towards the mountain in amazement.

The cavern in the mountain stood open and the children
came tumbling out. Every one of them! They came running
towards their parents, waving and laughing.
The Pied Piper came down too and he was smiling.
This is what he said:
'*You've punished the Mayor*
For breaking his word,
So here is the merriest
Tune ever heard!'

He began to play, and the people of Hamelin danced around
with their children for sheer happiness and joy.

The Pied Piper got his thousand guilders and went away.
The children were safely home and there was never a rat
to be seen again. So the lovely town of Hamelin became
a happy town at last.
But if you ever meet the Pied Piper, be sure to keep your word!

Oxford University Press, Walton Street, Oxford OX2 6DP

Oxford is a trade mark of Oxford University Press

Copyright © Val Biro 1985
This version first published 1985
Reprinted 1986, 1992
This edition first published 1997

All rights reserved.

A CIP catalogue record for this book is available from the British Library
ISBN 0 19 272321 9 (paperback)

Printed in Hong Kong